Giant Tales from Wales

Giant Tales
from Wales

Brenda Wyn Jones

A translation by Ann Saer

Illustrations by Peter Brown

First Impression—1998

ISBN 1 85902 588 9

© original text: Brenda Wyn Jones
© translation: Ann Saer
© illustrations: Peter Brown

This book is published with the support of the Arts Council of Wales.

Printed in Wales at
Gomer Press, Llandysul, Ceredigion

CONTENTS

Y CARNEDDAU

SNOWDON

BERWYN
MOUNTAINS

CADER IDRIS

SHREWSBURY

PUMLUMON
MOUNTAINS

PRESELI HILLS

BRIDE'S BAY

MILFORD
HAVEN

RHONDDA
VALLEY

RHYMNEY
VALLEY

1 The Giant of Snowdonia

There was once a giant called Rhitta who lived on the top of Snowdon, the highest mountain in Wales.

'Brr-r-r! It's cold up here!' roared Rhitta one winter's morning, shivering.

Of course it was cold. What did he expect if he insisted on living on the top of Snowdon in the middle of January? Rhitta did enjoy rambling over the mountains of Eryri in the snow, but often, as he strode from peak to peak, he nearly froze to death. His cave wasn't very warm either. Icy winds swirled around the wood fire, which was the only kind of central heating he could afford. Old Rhitta had a problem.

'I know what I'll do,' he said, after some thought.

Can you guess what he did? Well, he took hold of his great long beard, and wrapped it tightly round his head and shoulders, like a muffler.

'That's better,' he said, leaping across another valley to get a better view of Anglesey and the Menai Strait.

Rhitta was chief of the giants of north Wales. At that time, lots of giants lived there. Nearly all of them were very fierce and nasty, but not one of them was as fierce or as nasty as Rhitta. All the other giants were afraid of him and kept well away from Snowdon. Rhitta was a real old bully. He terrified the others just because he was bigger than they were and grumpier. And this

particular January morning, because he still felt chilly in spite of his enormous whiskery muffler, he began to rant and rage and generally work himself up into a gigantic temper.

'Dither-r-r-r-ing dr-r-r-r-rragons!' he blustered, shivering. 'My head and shoulders are beautifully warm, but every other bit of me is freezing. My feet feel like two blocks of ice. What a shame my beard isn't big enough to make a warm cloak. Drat and double-drat everything and everybody!'

Suddenly he had an idea. He would cut off the other giants' beards and make them into a cloak for himself. That would show them who was the boss. In any case, it wasn't such a dreadful thing to do—their beards would

grow again before they could say '*Mawredd-mawr-edrych-i-lawr-mae-rhywun-wedi-dwyn-fy-marf*' which is the Welsh for, 'Goodness-gracious-me-look-down-there-someone's-nicked-my-beard'. Better still, he would think up a cunning excuse to make each beard-cutting a punishment on the giant in question. His mind was made up.

The first giant to lose his beard was called Idris. As giants go, Idris was a gentle, innocent kind of chap. He had never done anybody any harm, and enjoyed living on his own in the Eryri mountains. His hobby was astronomy. He was perfectly happy, just star-gazing.

On this particular morning, Idris was quietly minding his own business, perched on a mountain-top near Dolgellau. He had sat there so often that he'd worn away the rock into a comfy hollow. All night he had studied the stars and now he felt ready for bed. Yawning widely, he stretched his arms high into the sky, and stood up. As he did so, he felt a sharp twinge of pain in his big toe.

'Aa-ww!' he yelled, bending down to see what was wrong. 'Ah—there's a stone in my shoe.' He winkled out the stone, picked it up and raised his arm, ready to fling it down the mountainside into the valley below.

'There!' he shouted. 'And a jolly good riddance to you, too. You'll never bother anyone on this mountain again.'

The next minute, he saw a huge shadow block out the sun—a shadow which crept nearer and nearer, and grew larger and larger. Yes, of course—it was Rhitta.

'Who is throwing stones at me?' roared Rhitta in a great, bellowing voice which made everything around tremble and shake. 'Did I hear you say "good riddance?" Is that what you said, you moon-faced rascal?'

'No! No! I mean . . . Yes, I did say "good riddance", but I was talking to the stone, not to you. I really am very sorry. I didn't see you. Honestly,' cried Idris, cowering.

'Come here,' shouted Rhitta, grasping Idris's beard with one hand and whipping an enormous pair of scissors out of his pocket with the other. 'This will teach you a lesson,' he said, snipping straight through the beard. He waved it under Idris's nose. 'Just you remember that I, Rhitta, am chief of all the giants, and no one is allowed to throw stones at me.'

Off he lumbered with a beard for his warm new cloak.

When the other giants heard what had happened to Idris, they were furious as well as alarmed. 'For shame,' they said. 'Fancy cutting off Idris's beard for no reason at all.' They all decided to lie low for a while, and keep out of Rhitta's way. But he was more powerful and more cunning than they were. One by one, he managed to cut off every single giant's beard, using the slightest of excuses each time. At last, while the others shivered, Rhitta had a beautifully warm and cosy cloak. He thoroughly enjoyed himself, showing it off.

'Fee-fo-fi-fum-diddle-dum-diddle-dum,' he said to himself one day. 'I am the chief of all the giants. Ho, ho, ho. And my cloak really is magnificent. It's funny, though—my right shoulder still feels chilly. I wonder why that is?' He bent his head to peer over his shoulder. There, in the cloak, was a large, bald gap.

'Oho! I shall have to get hold of another beard,' he said. 'And it will have be a very special one, so that I can finish off my cloak with a bold, eye-catching collar. Now, let me think. Who would have a beard that would fit the bill?'

Rhitta was faced with a problem now, because he had already shaved the beard of every single giant in Snowdonia, and not one had grown a new one yet. Then he heard about the great king Arthur who lived in the south. It was said that Arthur had a fantastic beard— thick and long and golden. Just what Rhitta wanted!

Perhaps you can guess what Rhitta did next. Yes. He sent a message to Arthur, demanding his beard as a present. Arthur sent a message back, stating that his beard was not available, but that he would find an even better one for Rhitta if he came down to collect it.

Rhitta was delighted to hear this. Off he went down to south Wales to meet King Arthur. He took a large army of soldiers with him, to frighten the king. But as they drew near Arthur's court, there was a sudden storm of thunder and lightning.

'What on earth is all that noise?' the soldiers asked fearfully. 'And what is that flashing light?' They were terrified by the din and dazzled by the flaring brightness.

'I know what's happening,' said one old warrior. 'It's the sound of Arthur's armies marching. The strange light in the sky is the sun, glittering on their weapons.'

When they heard this, Rhitta's soldiers ran for their lives back home to Snowdonia. But Rhitta didn't. He went on to meet the king. When at last he reached the court, Arthur himself came out to meet him.

'You promised me a beard even better than yours to finish off my cloak,' said Rhitta boldly, staring in admiration at Arthur's great beard.

'Yes, I did indeed. Come here,' said Arthur, grasping Rhitta's beard with one hand and slicing clean through it with his enormous, knife-sharp sword. 'Here you are, the best beard of all. This must be sewn on the hem.'

The old giant was heart-broken. 'But why ?' he cried.

'You've been behaving like a real old bully up there in the north, so I've heard. From now on, you will answer to *me*. Everybody will know that when they see your own beard dragging on the ground. Now, off you go back to Snowdon. And behave yourself, or else . . .'

And that is what happened. Rhitta had to behave himself after that. After all, there was no knowing what Arthur would do next time!

2 The Giant of the Rhondda

'I am the biggest!
I am the best!
I am the greatest in the whole wide world!'

Brag, brag, brag. That was all Hywel ever did from morning till night, day in day out. He wasn't half as nasty as old Rhitta, but he used to get on everyone's nerves because he was forever challenging the other giants to a fight. Everyone who lived in the Rhondda valley had had more than enough of him. It was always the same boring old chant:

'I am the biggest!
I am the best!
I am the greatest in the whole wide world!'

Of course, everybody used to agree with him because not one of them wanted to give him an excuse to give them a good hiding. But though he looked so nasty and threatening, really and truly Hywel, like so many bullies, was just a great big baby. And in the end, he showed off a bit too much. This is what happened.

Hywel had heard that there was a great giant in Ireland who terrified all the people in the land. In fact, it was said that this Irish giant really was the biggest, the best and the greatest giant in the whole world.

Do you know what Hywel did? He challenged the Irish giant to come over to the Rhondda to fight him. Of course, he thought the giant wouldn't take any notice of the invitation. Well—that's certainly what he hoped.

'After all, Ireland's far enough away over the sea,' Hywel reassured himself. 'Though I do remember hearing my father say that the great giant Bendigeidfran once walked from Wales to Ireland. But so what? Whoever heard of a giant from Ireland coming over here to Wales? He'll never come, that's for sure.'

Months went by and Hywel's head had grown bigger than ever.

'I must be a super-giant,' he said to everyone. 'Why, even the great giant of Ireland is too scared to come over here to fight me.

> 'I am the biggest!
> I am the best!
> I am the greatest in the whole wide world!
> I am a SUPER-GIANT!'

All the people of the Rhondda were really fed up with his boasting, but were too frightened to disagree.

Then, one morning, as Hywel was sitting outside the door of his cottage, waiting for his wife to bring him his breakfast, he saw a huge shape in the distance, moving slowly towards him.It grew bigger and bigger as it came closer. YES! It was the giant from Ireland. He was so enormous that he looked like a great mountain moving up the valley, and his eyes glittered like twin lakes in the morning sun. Hywel fled into the house in terror and squeezed himself under the table.

'What on earth's the matter with you?' asked his wife.

'It's the giant from Ireland!' cried Hywel. 'Here . . . now!'

'But I thought you said you were looking forward to meeting him?'

'Yes, yes, I know, but just go over to the window and look at the size of him. Oh, whatever shall I do?'

'I know,' said his wife, after thinking for a moment. 'I have an idea. Go upstairs and hide under the bed.'

'But he'll be bound to find me there!' Hywel protested.

'Do as I tell you,' said his wife, 'and perhaps I can save you. You really are a very silly giant, making all this trouble for yourself.'

'Yes, you're right, I know that now,' Hywel snivelled. 'But if you save me, I'll never, ever brag and show off again. That's a promise.'

'Cross your heart? Honest to goodness?' asked his wife hopefully. She was tired of hearing how marvellous he was, and how lucky she was to have married him.

'Cross-my-heart-and-honest-to-goodness-and-really-and-truly-for-ever-Amen,' said Hywel.

'Right!' said his wife. 'Now move—fast. Give me your shoes and go upstairs to hide.'

Hywel crept upstairs and crawled under their enormous bed, his heart pounding like a grandfather clock and his legs quivering like jellies. Meanwhile, his wife had grabbed his shoes and set them carefully in front of the fire. Then she took her time over preparing breakfast.

'The top of the mornin' to you an' all! Is there a welcome here for Gwyddel, a giant from Ireland?' roared a lilting Irish voice at the door.

'Of course you are welcome here, Gwyddel. Come in,' said Hywel's wife, smiling at him nicely. 'You're just in time to join us for breakfast. We'll be more than happy to share it with you when Hywel comes home.'

'Aha,' said Gwyddel. 'He'll be the person I've come all this way to see. And where would he be then? In bed, perhaps?' And he glanced at the enormous pair of shoes warming in front of the fire.

'In bed? No indeed,' she retorted indignantly, staring at him straight in the eye. 'But he'll be delighted to see you. I know he's looking forward to meeting you.'

'Oh, is he? Well, we'll have to see about that. But what are these doing here?' asked Gwyddel, pointing to the shoes on the hearth. 'Does Hywel usually go

20

hunting in his bare feet? I can't believe that, somehow. But I'll tell you what I do believe—there's an old show-off hiding somewhere in this house because he's too much of a baby to face me.'

'No, you're quite wrong there,' insisted the good wife.

'Who do these shoes belong to, then?

'Oh, they're the baby's shoes,' she replied. ' The *cariad bach* is asleep in his cot upstairs.'

Gwyddel the giant of Ireland stared at the shoes. He began to think hard. 'Connemara!' he said to himself. 'If the baby's as big as this, his dad must be . . . massive.'

'Er—Missus,' he said aloud, his voice trembling. 'I've just remembered . . . two important appointments I have to get back for. There's an important committee I have to attend in Tipperary, and there's a gig in Galway. I don't know how they slipped my mind. I shall have to hurry back at once. Tell your husband how sorry I am to have missed him . . . nice meeting you . . .'

The giant of Ireland backed out of the door like a dog with its tail between its legs and stumbled headlong down the valley to Cardiff Bay. He was determined to get far away before Hywel arrived home.

'Hywel! You can come downstairs to have your breakfast now,' called his wife.

'Are you sure he's gone?' quavered Hywel from his cwtsh under the bed.

'Yes—and he'll never come back either,' she laughed.

'Thank goodness for that,' said Hywel happily and straightaway he began to chant:

> 'I am the biggest!
> I am the best!
> I am the great . . .'

'Stop that nonsense at once,' said his wife, sharp as a kitchen knife. 'Just you remember what you promised. If you ever brag like that again, I'll tell everybody what really happened when Gwyddel came by!'

'Oh, all right then,' Hywel agreed, hanging his head and sulking. He'd been looking forward to telling his own version of the story to the other giants.

From that day on, Hywel really did stop boasting. He was too afraid that his wife would tell the true story of how she had got rid of Gwyddel, the great giant of Ireland, all by herself.

3 The Giant of the Carneddau

Fflur was a very pretty young girl—but she was always lonely. Her father was a nasty old giant called Idwal, who made her stay in the castle all the time to look after him, instead of letting her go out to make friends. He would never even let her go shopping. So she had no friends at all, poor dab. Day after day, there she was, cooking his meals, washing and ironing his breeches and jerkins, his pants and vests, and trying to keep the old castle clean. She tried to keep her father clean too, but old Idwal hated soap and water.

No one ever dared come near the gloomy castle in the Carneddau mountains because Idwal was such a fierce giant. He was more terrifying than even Ysbaddaden Bencawr, and everyone knows how much trouble Olwen his daughter had with him. There was another reason too why people didn't like going near Idwal. Can you guess what it was? Yes, of course. He SMELLED! Fflur tried her best with him but he hated water so much, Idwal never, ever washed, let alone had a bath.

One day, Fflur went out to the meadows outside the castle to pick blackberries and get some fresh air. Her father loved blackberry tart, and she thought perhaps he would be nicer to her if she made him a blackberry tart for his pudding after dinner.

As she was picking the blackberries, a handsome young man happened to be passing by. He noticed that she was a very pretty young girl, and said, 'Hello. My name's Ffrancon. What's your name?'

'Fflur,' she answered, looking down shyly, but peeping at him from under her eyelashes because she had never in her life seen such a good-looking lad before.

'Fflur. That means flower, doesn't it? It really suits you. Can you help me? I'm on my way to the town, but somehow, I've managed to get lost.' Ffrancon smiled at her. 'Could you show me the way, please?

'Of course I can,' said Fflur, blushing happily.

She told him exactly how to get to the town, and then they carried on chatting together.

'Oh—I shall have to go home,' said Fflur at last. 'It's nearly dinner-time and my father will be cross if his dinner's not on the table ready for him.'

'May I come back tomorrow to talk to you?' asked Ffrancon.

'Certainly you may,' said Fflur, 'but we'll have to make sure my father doesn't see us.'

And after that, the two of them met every day. The old giant began to get a bit tired of blackberry tart, even though he was so fond of it.

'Fflur, will you marry me?' asked Ffrancon one morning. By now, he had fallen head-over-heels in love with her. 'Come on. We'll go up to the castle to see your father so that I can ask him for your hand in marriage. I'm sure he isn't as bad as you say he is.'

'Oh no, don't do that, 'said Fflur, fearful even though she was very happy about the idea of marrying Ffrancon. 'My dad is a really nasty, spiteful old giant. He'll be sure to do something awful to you. There can be no hope of us ever getting married!'

She began to weep. But Ffrancon loved her very much and was determined to marry her. 'Don't cry,' he said. 'I'll tell you what we'll do. We'll run away without telling him. You pack everything ready and come here first thing tomorrow morning, and I'll borrow a strong horse. Then we can escape from his clutches for ever!'

In the end, Fflur agreed, for she loved this fine young man and wanted so much to leave Idwal forever. But still she worried, because she knew her father was also a magician who knew all about magic spells and charms. He would be bound to follow and catch them.

'I know!' she said to herself next morning as she packed her bag, ready to run away with Ffrancon. On tiptoe, very softly and quietly, she crept into her father's bedroom to find three special things that belonged to him—a comb, a razor and a mirror. They were all three full of magic, and she hoped they would help the pair of them to escape. She found them quickly and hid them in her bag. Then off she went to join Ffrancon.

When Idwal came home and found his dinner wasn't on the table, he was furious. 'Where's that lazy judy of a daughter of mine?' he bellowed, raging and swearing and terrifying everybody around. He roared through the castle searching every nook and cranny, but there was no sign of Fflur anywhere. 'Fetch me a horse!' he

shouted to a servant. 'I shall find her and bring her back!'

By this time, Fflur and Ffrancon were miles away. As they galloped like the wind, further and further from the castle and Idwal, Fflur happened to glance over her shoulder. Who should she see in the distance but her father, on his great horse, travelling far more swiftly than they were, and coming closer and closer by the minute.

'Take this!' said Fflur. She opened her bag, seized the comb and flung it down behind her. In the place where the comb fell, at once there sprang up a forest of soaring trees and thick, thorny brambles. She could hear her father shouting in the distance, but he couldn't push his way through the forest.

By the time Idwal had hacked his way with his sword through the trees and bushes, Fflur and Ffrancon were miles away again. But when she looked back after a while, there was Idwal once more, galloping swiftly towards them.

'Take this!' said Fflur for the second time. She took the razor from her bag and threw it down behind her. At once, a vast range of mountains appeared, mountains far too high for even a giant to climb. Fflur and Ffrancon could hear him bellowing faintly in the distance as they swept onwards.

Though it took hours, in the end Idwal managed to tunnel right through the mountains by scraping away at the the rock and earth with his bare hands. The next time Fflur looked back, there he was again, close on their heels.

'Oh no!' she thought. 'I have only one thing left.' She grabbed the mirror from her bag and threw it down behind her.

As soon as it reached the ground, the magic mirror changed into a wide lake which stretched as far as the eye could see. This, time, Idwal was mad with rage and terror, because he couldn't bear water. He wrenched wildly at his horse's reins, startling the poor creature so much that it reared up on its hind legs and threw him right into the middle of the lake. There, he drowned, and that was the end of the giant.

Fflur was free at last to marry her handsome young man. She and Ffrancon lived happily ever after, and she was never lonely again. But every time Fflur combed her hair and looked at herself in the mirror, and every time Ffrancon looked in the mirror when he was shaving, they used to remember Idwal, the wicked old giant of Carneddau.

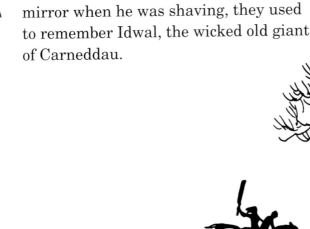

4 The Giant of the Preseli Hills

'What shall we do? What on earth shall we do?'

Once upon a time, this was the question on the lips of all the humans and fairies who lived around Haverfordwest in Pembrokeshire. Not one of them could remember such a storm at sea, such a wild tempest of a storm. Huge waves battered and drowned the ships in St. Bride's bay and flooded the cottages nearest to the shores.

Do you know how the storm had begun? It was all the fault of two monsters who had started fighting out at sea. They were particularly revolting creatures to look at—like two slimy, slithering serpents. As they fought, the water seethed around them like a cauldron of boiling *cawl*. They twisted and turned on the sea-bed, churning up mud and sand which was flung on to the shore, and began to block up the mouth of the two rivers called the Cleddau. And the sea-monsters' tails whipped angrily to and fro in the water, creating great waves which thudded and crashed on to the beaches around the bay.

Everybody was miserable. Everything being ruined by the storm, and every day the situation seemed to be getting worse. There was no sign of an end to the fight. At last, the people and fairies called a joint committee meeting to discuss the matter. But though they all talked for hours, nobody had the faintest idea how to solve the problem. They were about to go home when Moelyn, the oldest of the dwarves, made a suggestion.

'How about asking the giant of the Preseli Hills to help us?' he said.

Surely that was a very strange idea—fancy asking a giant to help! People usually run for their lives if a giant's about. But the giant of Preseli was supposed to be a very kind, friendly giant, quite unlike Rhitta, or Idwal and most of the others.

'But no one's seen him for years . . .'

'They say he only wakes up once in a hundred years . . .'

He' s asleep somewhere in a cave on Foel Drygarn . . .'

'We'll never find him . . .'

Everyone was talking at once. Then up piped a small voice from the back: 'Moelyn is right. We really have no other choice. Come on—let's go and look for the giant and ask him to come and help us.'

Moelyn turned round to see who was speaking. 'Thank you, Mymryn,' he said, smiling kindly at the smallest (and wisest) of the fairies present. 'I knew you'd agree that this is the only thing left for us to do.'

Everyone had heard their grandmothers and grandfathers talk about the warm-hearted giant of the Preseli Hills. He would be bound to help them again, they felt sure. The problem was, where could he be

31

found? Off they went to look for his cave in the hills. They searched and searched for days, but there was no sign of the cave where the giant was sleeping. Then, one afternoon, as he clambered up the hill called Foel Cwmcerwyn, Mymryn heard a strange noise coming from under his feet. 'Hey, wait!' he shouted. 'There's something very odd here. Listen.'

When they heard the distant rumbling sound inside the hillside, they were all frightened. 'It's an earthquake!' cried one fairy.

'Run for your life!' yelled another.

'Wait,' said Mymryn, crossly. The ground under our feet isn't moving at all. It can't be an earthquake. The cave where the old giant is sleeping must be

underneath us, and that strange rumbling has to be the sound of his snoring. Let's go and look for the entrance.'

They all rushed to search the mountainside for the way into the cave. In the end, hidden under a large tussock of heather, they found the mouth of a tunnel which opened into an enormous cavern. 'Mymryn, you were right—this is where the giant is,' they said. 'Let's wake him up!'

But this wasn't so easy. The giant was fast asleep in the part of the cave furthest from the entrance, snoring so loudly that they had to put their hands over their ears as they drew closer. 'Wake up! Wake up, giant!' they shouted all together at the top of their voices. But he didn't stir. So they all shouted again: 'Wake up! Wake up, Preseli giant!'

The giant still slept on. So some of the fairies leaped on to his chest, others jumped on his head and on to his shoulders, and a few of them bounded up and down on his great fat belly. One or two of the boldest fairies hung on to his thick, hairy beard, and swung to and fro. He still didn't budge. They yelled again, but their voices were so shrill and piping, the giant couldn't hear them, even when Mymryn and another fairy ventured right inside his ear to shout.

'Wait a minute, said Mymryn at last. 'I know what we'll do.'

He took a feather from his cap and began to tickle the giant's nose. After a minute or two, it began to twitch slowly from side to side, and the giant lifted his big hand to rub it.

'Careful! Get out of the way, everyone, warned Mymryn. 'He's going to snee . . .'

'a - a - a - a - a - a - a — a — — a a a a a a a a a a a a a a a — AAAAATISHSHSHOOOoooo!'

Luckily, they all managed to scramble headlong round the corner of a large clump of stalagmites before the giant finally sneezed, or they would have been blown to Milford Haven.

The giant opened an enormous eye and looked about him, surprised. 'Who is this interrupting my nap?' he asked sleepily. 'Is it little mice I can hear skittering around in the darkness?'

'No,' said Mymryn bravely, trying to speak in a deep bass voice. 'It's us, the fairies and dwarves. We're local. I really am very sorry to have to disturb you, but we do need your help.'

'But it surely isn't time yet?' asked the giant.

'No, it isn't. We know that. But please, will you help us? We're in great trouble down in St Bride's bay.'

'And what is your problem?' By now, the giant had opened both eyes and was listening to them attentively.

Everybody started to talk at once about the sea-monsters and the storms and the disasters around the Pembrokeshire coast.

'Hisht, hisht,' laughed the giant, unable to make head or tail of the story. 'You're just like little mice with your squealing and squeaking. Let's go down to the shore to see exactly what the trouble is.'

The fairies and dwarves climbed into his pockets, hanging out and waving to their friends in excitement as the giant strode from the mountain-top down to the seashore. Even with the extra weight of the fairies, he covered the ground in just ten strides. He could see for himself how the coast and countryside nearest the beaches had been ruined by the storms. Everywhere, brown mud lay in untidy heaps on the fields, as if giant moles had been tunnelling there. Huge mounds of silt and sand had choked the Cleddau estuary. The giant looked around him, horrified. He carefully set down his small friends—who had thoroughly enjoyed their journey. Then he went over to the river mouth and stood astride the estuary. Bending down, he lifted up great handfuls of the mud and threw it out of the way on to the Preseli hills.

At once, the water started to flow with a rush back into the bay. The giant was busy for hours, bending and stretching as he cleared away the mess.

'There, my small friends,' he said at last, wiping away
the perspiration on his forehead with a hanky as big as
a tablecloth, and dislodging one elderly dwarf who had
fallen asleep in the giant's pocket on the way down. 'I

am really looking forward to going back to sleep after all that hard work.'

'But the two monsters are still fighting!' said Mymryn. 'Look at those waves!'

And then, that very minute, the sea suddenly became calm. Everyone gaped as one glistening sea-monster heaved out of the depths and swam, straight as an arrow, out to the distant horizon. They gazed and gazed for hours, but there was no sign of the other sea-creature. The battle was over at last.

'Hooray!' shouted the people and fairies together. 'Hip hip hooray, Preseli giant. You've saved us all again. Thank you so much. We are very grateful.'

'That's all right,' said the giant amiably, grinning a wide and toothy grin, and stretching his arms above his head. 'Oh, I feel really exhausted now. I shall go back to bed. Remember, don't wake me up for another hundred years.'

'Farewell! Thank you again!' said the joyful crowd of people and fairies as they watched him take the ten strides back from the seashore to Foel Cwmcerwyn and his cave. They all felt very happy, though they were sad to see him go. No one ever saw the giant of the Preseli Hills again. But it's said you can still see his giant footprints on either side of the Cleddau estuary, where he bent down to clear the mud. Don't forget to look out for them if you ever go down to Pembrokeshire.

5 The Giant of the Rhymney Valley

Long ago, the Rhymney Valley was an especially happy place to live. Everybody used to enjoy singing and dancing, particularly the fairies. Then, it all changed. The singing and dancing stopped, and the people and fairies became gloomy and sad. And all because a nasty giant had come to live in Gilfach Fargod, to a tall tower there, surrounded by a big garden. Everyone was afraid of this giant because he had a name for catching and killing his victims—both innocent people and un-suspecting fairies that came his way. Everyone with any sense tried very hard to keep clear of him.

He was so hideously ugly to look at that even old giant Rhitta was afraid of him. Worse still, it was almost impossible to avoid being seen by him because he had one eye on his forehead and the other on the back of his head. He could see in *all* directions. To top it all, he carried a huge stick with a poisonous snake entwined around it. It really wasn't surprising that people jumped at their own shadows and always went about their business as stealthily as mice—especially the children.

But there was one brave lad who was determined to slay the Cwm Rhymni giant. Ianto was ten years old and had lived all his life with his mother at the edge of the forest. He had a very good reason to hate the giant. One day, his mother had gone out to collect firewood from the forest and had never come back. Though weeks had gone by, and Ianto had searched everywhere around, there was no sign of her anywhere.

'The giant of the Rhymney Valley must have found her and killed her,' said Ianto to himself. 'I must get rid of him so that everyone can be happy again. I don't think I've any hope of getting Mam back, but I will go to the Queen of the Fairies to ask for her help. She'll be bound to know what to do.'

That night, instead of going to bed, Ianto crept out into the woods to look for the Fairy Queen. But where could she be? He wandered for hours without seeing anybody. He was about to give up when he suddenly remembered something his mother had said to him.

'I know. I remember Mam showing me exactly where the fairies used to dance in the days before the giant ruined everything. I'll go there to have a look.'

He went through the woods to the little green glade his mother had shown him. Yes—there she was, the queen of the fairies, sitting on a rock almost as if she were expecting him. 'So you've come at last, Ianto,' she said, in a voice like a tiny silver bell. 'Good. How can I help you?'

'Can you help me to slay the giant of Cwm Rhymni? I'm so lonely, and it's all his fault. He killed my mother and I'm all alone now.'

'I don't know anything about that,' said the Fairy

Queen, looking at him kindly, 'But I do know who can help you.'

'Who? Who?' Ianto asked, frantic to find out.

'Have you noticed the owl who hoots in the great oak tree on the edge of the forest?'

'Yes, she's been there ever since I lost Mam. The sound of her hooting is so mournful, it breaks my heart and keeps me awake every night.'

'She will know what to do. You go to the owl and ask her to help you.'

'Go to the owl? But how can she possibly help?'

'Do as I say and you'll see.'

'But I shan't be able to understand what she says.'

'In that case, I'll have to come with you.'

And off they went through the forest to have a word with the owl before sunrise.

'Owl, Owl, how can you get rid of the giant of Cwm Rhymni?' asked the fairy queen.

'Too-whit, too-whoo. Too-whit, too-whoo . . .' the owl began to speak. Ianto listened to her intently, but he couldn't understand a word she was saying.

'Thank you, Owl,' said the Fairy Queen at last. 'Listen Ianto, this is what she says . . .

A bow and arrow set in the tree,
Will slay the giant of Cwm Rhymni.'

'A bow and arrow in the tree?' said Ianto in bewilderment. 'I don't understand, at all, how that can help . . .'

'You do exactly what the owl says and you will see.'

'Oh, all right,' said Ianto, disappointed. He really couldn't see how exactly the owl's plan could work, but he was ready to try anything.

Ianto hurried home to search the cottage for his grandfather's bow and arrow. It was a fine, strong bow, and luckily there were plenty of arrows left in the leather bag which hung behind the door. Ianto chose two sharp arrows, just in case whoever was going to try to slay the giant missed with the first shot. He had to risk going out again into the forest, though by now it was almost daybreak. Fortunately, there was no sign of the giant, though Ianto knew he used to walk that way often during the day. Neither was there any sign of the owl in the branches of the oak tree. Ianto guessed she would be fast asleep somewhere, perhaps inside the tree-trunk.

'There, little owl,' he said, placing the bow and two arrows firmly in the branches. 'I don't know how this will help, but this is what you said—

A bow and arrow set in the tree
will slay the giant of Cwm Rhymni'

And he hurried home in case the giant should happen to catch him.

Later in the day, after a delicious meat-and-gravy dinner, the giant went out of his tower in Gilfach Fargod and wandered off towards the forest to meet his girlfriend. Yes, indeed, the old giant did have a girlfriend, even though he was the ugliest creature on the face of the earth. But remember, she wasn't exactly a work of art herself. Erchyllwen was in fact utterly hideous, an ugly old crone. But the giant thought the world of her and believed that she was the most beautiful girl who'd ever walked on this earth.

'I wonder where darling Erchyllwen is?' he thought to himself after waiting for some time under the oak tree. That was where they used to meet nearly every day. The old witch was usually the first to arrive. After all, her magic broomstick could whisk her there in a flash. She didn't need to walk anywhere.

'Oh, I do feel tired,' said the giant to the snake, which hissed at him softly. 'Let's sit under the tree to wait for her. I don't expect she'll be too long.' He lowered his large backside to the ground with a crash that made the earth tremble for miles around. The people of the valley thought it was an earthquake and were very frightened.

The sun was hot and soon the giant fell asleep. When he began to snore loudly, the owl came out of her snug

little hole in the oak tree. She found the bow and arrow that Ianto had set in its branches and held it tightly in her claw. Then, very carefully, using her beak, she set an arrow in the bow and aimed straight at the old giant's heart.

Whish! The arrow whistled through the air, reaching its mark and killing the giant instantly. Strangely, that same moment, the serpent slithered off the stick like a limp piece of string into a motionless heap on the ground. It too was dead.

'Hooray!' shouted the fairies, who had hidden in the trees to watch. 'That's the end of the giant of Cwm Rhymni and the nasty old snake!'

But before they had a chance to celebrate, a great

black shadow rocketed down through the trees. It was Erchyllwen, the old witch, who had come to look for her boyfriend. 'Oh, my dearest love!' she howled, when she found him lying there with an arrow through his heart. 'Who has done this to you? If I hadn't been waiting for the cauldron to boil, I'd have been here earlier. Oh, what shall I do?' And she bent down to listen to his chest in case his heart was still beating.

The owl hopped silently along the branch, grasped the bow with her claw and picked up the second arrow with her beak.

Whish! The arrow whistled through the air and hit

the old crone in her head. She fell to the ground with a great thump, quite dead.

'Hooray! Hooray!' yelled the fairy folk, this time besides themselves with joy, and dancing and singing with delight.

'What's all that noise about?' wondered Ianto as he heard the commotion from the direction of the forest. 'I wonder . . . Oh, I do hope . . .'

He ran as fast as he could towards the source of the noise. There he saw a scene he would never forget— hundreds of fairies dancing and singing in a circle around the bodies of the old giant and the old witch, lying there like a two-humped mountain.

'Come here, Ianto,' said the Fairy Queen. He stepped shyly towards her. 'Thanks to you, we are rid of the giant and the witch at last.'

'But I didn't do anything. I only put the bow in the tree as the owl had told me to do. So who killed the giant?'

'The owl, of course. Come here, little owl.'

The owl fluttered quietly out of the tree and perched in front of the queen. The queen raised her magic wand and waved it three times around the little owl's head. In a blinding flash, the owl had vanished. There, in her place, stood Ianto's mother, smiling at him.

'I am so sorry, Ianto,' said the Fairy Queen. 'I had to turn your mother into an owl so that she could escape from the giant's clutches. He nearly caught her that day when she got lost in the forest. And I couldn't undo the magic until she had slain the giant. Only you could help her to do that.'

Everyone in the Rhymney Valley was happy that day, and there was nobody happier than Ianto and his mother.

But that wasn't the end of the story. After a few weeks, the bodies of the giant and the witch began to smell even worse than the giant Idwal, and that really is saying something. The stench wafted across the land like the smell of a thousand bad eggs, making all the people hold their breath as well as their noses!

'We'll never get rid of this stink unless we bury the bodies,' said the people. They dug a huge hole in the ground and dumped the two smelly corpses inside. This was not an easy task. It took twenty cart-horses and yards of rope before they finally succeeded.

So that was the problem solved? I hear you ask. No, indeed. The stench wafted up through the earth. It was worse than ever. In fact it was so bad that many of the people and the fairies began to think they would have to move away from the area.

'How about cremating the bodies then?' said someone at last. So they set about building an immense bonfire. That bonfire was really something to remember—the flames leaped high into the air and it gave out so much heat that it made everyone sweat pints. By nightfall, all that was left of the bodies of the giant and witch was a pile of grey ashes. But the bonfire went on burning.

'Hurry! Fetch water—quickly! The rocks near the bonfire are on fire!' Burning rocks? No one had heard of such a thing—but it was perfectly true. They put out the flames at last with buckets of water from the river. One man was brave enough to go and examine the rocks to see what had caused the fire.

'Here, the rock is black and shiny,' he said. 'That is what was burning. Look for yourself at these chunks of rock.'

Everyone took bits of the black rock home to put on their fires. They were delighted. The black stones were much better than firewood and burned with a steady red glow. From that day onwards, they all went down every day to the pit where the bonfire had been to hew the black rock instead of going to the forest to collect firewood.

And that, they say, is how coal came to be discovered in the Rhymney Valley.

47

6 The Giant of the Berwyn Mountains

The giant of the Berwyn mountains was dog-tired.

'Where on earth is that place they call Shrewsbury?' he grumbled. 'I've been on the road for hours and my feet are really sore. A—aaw!'

It was only that morning that the giant had made up his mind that he was going to walk to Shrewsbury. Why do you think he wanted to go there? He'd certainly heard enough about the town. Oh, yes, indeed he had—quite enough. And that morning, he decided it was time to do what a giant had to do, and go there.

'Nasty people live in Shrewsbury. Naughty, *wicked* people,' he muttered to himself for the hundredth time.

It was the people of Shrewsbury who had slain his old father long ago for no reason at all. His poor old dad hadn't done anything wrong, except for borrowing a fat cow for his supper now and again from the meadows on the banks of the river Severn.

'They shall pay for what they did to my daddy,' said the Berwyn giant to himself that morning as he dug the garden, lifting a clod of earth on to his enormous spade. 'I know what I'll do. I can carry enough soil on my spade to block up the river Severn and make a huge dam. Then the water will overflow the town and drown all the people. Ho ho—that will be fun. I'll get them in the end!'

He heaved a mountain of soil on to his spade and set off to Shrewbury. But he had no idea where Shrewsbury was. Giants aren't usually very clever, even though they are so big, and the giant of the Berwyn mountains was no different from the others. He couldn't read a map, and he couldn't ask anybody how to get there before starting off because no one would go anywhere near him—they were all too frightened.

'Oh, I'm lost,' he said at last, after walking for miles. 'And there hasn't been a soul around that I could have asked for directions.'

Naturally, people had stayed out of his way when they had heard he was on the road. They could hear the distant thunder of his feet and feel the ground tremble and shake as he came closer. If the foolish old giant had only known it, he had long since travelled past Shrewsbury town, and he was now well on his way into England. He sat down for a short break and to rest his arms after carrying the spade. As he gazed into the distance, he saw a little man with a sack on his back coming towards him.

'Thank goodness,' thought the giant. 'Here's someone coming at last. Perhaps he will know the way.'

The little man was a cobbler who used to walk to Shrewsbury every week to look for work. Since he was a good craftsman, lots of people used to bring him their shoes to mend. He was on his way home at the time, walking hunched up with his head down because of the heavy load on his back. So he hadn't noticed the giant. The sack was full of pairs of shoes he was taking home to repair by the next week.

The poor man had quite a shock when he heard a great voice booming across the country. 'Do you know where Shrewsbury is? Do I have much further to go?'

The cobbler dropped the sack in fright and looked up at the giant's legs. 'Cato'n pawb!' he said to himself. 'Those two mountains weren't there this morning when I was on my way to Shrewsbury.'

He got out his spectacles and put them on his nose so that he could see more clearly. When he realised that one of the 'mountains' was the leg of an enormous giant, sitting there in front of him, he felt quite faint with terror. He had never ever met a giant before and his first thought was that he should run for his life. Giants were usually very nasty. Though, come to think of it, he thought, this one doesn't look too bad. He's just sitting down, looking a bit pale. He's probably tired. And he is smiling rather nicely at me.

Then the cobbler noticed another mountain at the giant's side. It seemed to be a huge pile of earth, lying on an enormous spade. How odd!

'Who are you, and why do you want to go to Shrewsbury?' asked the cobbler, trying to sound as if he spoke to giants every day.

'I am the giant of the Berwyn mountains, and I want to go to Shrewsbury to get even with the people who live there. I want revenge!'

'Revenge? Whatever have they done?'

'The people of Shrewsbury killed my father long ago. I want to avenge my father's death.'

'But what are you going to do to them?' The cobbler was beginning to get worried now, thinking of all the people who brought him their shoes to mend every month.

'Do you see the earth on this spade? I'm going to throw it into the river Severn, and dam up the river until it overflows its banks and drowns the whole town. That's what I'm going to do. What d'you think of that?'

Not much, to be honest, thought the cobbler, realising how poor he would be if he lost all his customers. Then he noticed again how tired the giant looked. 'Well,' he

said, after thinking for a moment, 'you won't get to Shrewsbury today, that's for sure.'

'Why? Is it that far away from here?'

'Oh, yes, even for a big giant like yourself. I'm on my way back from the town myself, as it happens, and I've been on the road for weeks. See this sack? Look—it's loaded with old pairs of shoes. I've worn through them all, on my way back from Shrewsbury.'

The giant looked at the holes in the shoes, amazed. 'Dear me. It must be a very long way from here,' he said to the cobbler. 'What a good thing I met you. I'm already exhausted. I couldn't possibly face another long journey.'

'What will you do now?' asked the cobbler anxiously.

'I shall go home. But I'm not going to carry all this earth back with me.' And the giant picked up his spade and flung the pile of earth down on to the floor of the valley. The cobbler stared in surprise at the new mountain which had appeared so suddenly. Then the giant, who was tidy about some things, scraped off the mud from his boots and threw it beside the mountain, making another little hill by its side.

Feeling very disappointed, the giant lumbered slowly home to the Berwyn mountains. He never went anywhere near Shrewsbury town after that, so he never had a chance to dam up the river Severn or do anything to the people there. But he did leave his mark on Shropshire, for the mountain and the hillock are still there, they say.

7 The Giant of Pumlumon

'Who's that knocking on my door so late?' growled the giant of Pumlumon.

'It's me,' said a reedy little voice. 'I've been lost for hours on the mountains, and it's pitch dark outside. May I come in?'

'Of course you can come in! You're welcome,' said the giant, opening the door wide with a smile. With two smiles, actually, since this giant had two heads. He was delighted when he saw a small boy at the door, because he had nothing in the pantry for tomorrow's lunch. With a bit of gravy and stuffing, the boy would make a very tasty snack. 'Come in, come in . . . and what are you called, now?'

'My name's Jack,' said the boy, stepping bravely into the giant's castle.

The giant thought the boy would have been afraid of him. Everybody else was! But he didn't know Jack. He didn't know that Jack had already got rid of two giants already—one in Cornwall, where Jack lived, and another on his way to Wales. By now, Jack was famous as a giant-killer and he was looking forward to getting rid of this one as well.

'Come to the table,' invited one of the giant's heads warmly.

'Yes,' said the other head. 'There's plenty to eat.'

'No, thank you,' said Jack, though he was nearly starving. One glance at the giant's supper was enough. He sat watching the giant gobble up two huge bowls of greasy, fatty *cawl*, one for each head. When he was full, the giant wiped his two mouths on his sleeve and belched loudly .

'You look tired, my lad,' said one head.

'Come on, it's time for you to go to bed,' said the other.

Jack followed the giant up the dark staircase and as he went, he heard the two mouths whispering to each other.

'He'll make a tasty bite for lunch tomorrow . . .'

'. . . But we'll wait for him to go to sleep first.'

At the top of the stairs, the giant opened a great oak door.

'Here you are, this is your bedroom . . .'

'. . . Don't worry if you hear a noise in the night . . .'

'. . . That's when the rats come out to prowl around the castle . . .'

'. . . but they won't do you any harm.'

'Oh, don't worry about me—I'll be fine,' said Jack cheerfully. 'I'm so tired, I just can't keep my eyes open.'

'Very good, then . . .'

'. . . and good night,' chorused the giant's two heads, smiling two sly grins.

Jack, of course, had no intention of sleeping. Instead, he put a large block of wood on the mattress, under the bedclothes. Then he hid behind a cupboard. Hours went by while he did his best to keep awake.

At last, he heard the clock downstairs strike midnight, and then came the sound of giant footsteps creaking their way up the wooden staircase. The bedroom door opened softly. There stood the giant, with a candle in one hand and a huge club in the other. He tiptoed over to the bed and walloped it so hard with the club that little bits of wood flew into the air.

'He must have had very brittle bones,' said one head.

'Oh, his flesh will be tasty enough, you'll see,' said the other.

Next morning, the giant couldn't believe his four eyes when Jack walked into the kitchen, cool as a cucumber.

'Er, good morning, Jack . . .'

'. . . Did you sleep well?'

'Yes, thank you,' said Jack.

'What about the rats . . .?'

'. . . Didn't they disturb you?'

'No, not really. I thought I felt a rat's tail tickle my nose round about midnight, that's all.'

The giant's heads looked at each other in consternation. This boy must surely be exceptionally strong. Ah, well—-there would be plenty of other opportunities . . .

'Well, come and sit down with us. Have a bowl of porridge . . .'

'. . . A strong boy like you needs a good breakfast . . .'

Jack stared at the huge bowl of porridge. There must have been at least two litres there, but he didn't want the giant to think he was too puny to finish it all. The giant, of course, had two bowls in front of him, one for each mouth.

Jack began to eat. As the bowl rapidly emptied, the giant's four eyes grew round with surprise. Who would have thought that such a sprout of a lad could eat so much?

But the giant didn't know that Jack was scooping up the porridge in his spoon, making slurping swallowing noises and then pouring it all into a leather bag hidden under his coat.

'Thank you very much,' said Jack at last, scraping the bowl clean. 'That was absolutely delicious. And now, I'd like to show you a funny trick. I promise you, you'll split your sides laughing.'

'Right-ho . . .' said one head, eagerly.

'. . . I do love funny tricks,' said the other.

Jack whipped out a sharp knife and slit a large rent in the leather bag. The porridge spilled out all over the floor. The giant's two mouths opened in two great round O's of amazement.

'Huh, easy-peasy,' said the heads together, thinking that Jack had split his own stomach. The giant grabbed the knife and plunged it into his own belly, expecting his porridge also to flow out. Both heads screamed in agony as the giant crashed to the ground.

And that is how Jack the giant-killer got rid of the giant of Pumlumon. Yes, the old giant did split his sides—but not by laughing!